ANTHOLOGY OF SENTIMENTS

Avantika Chandra

Clever Fox
PUBLISHING

Chennai • Bangalore

CLEVER FOX PUBLISHING
Chennai, India

Published by CLEVER FOX PUBLISHING 2022
Copyright © Avantika Chandra 2022

All Rights Reserved.
ISBN: 978-93-56481-68-8

"My sentiments are like a poetry. Fewer words, deeper meanings..."

– Avantika

Anthology
of Sentiments

Index Table

Shades Of Roses

Darling, I know you always wonder
Why I bring you a bouquet of roses
Of different colors.
It's because your singularity can't be confined
By one color.
Your smile is as bright as a yellow rose,
You're a pure soul like a white rose,
A red rose reminds me of your solemn love,
A pink rose shows your playful side.
Like blue and black roses,
Sometimes you're calm,
Sometimes you're wild…
You see?
One shade of rose is not enough to describe you
So, I bring you a rainbow.

Lost Smile

When I sat beneath the sky
In search of my lost smile,
You smiled at me
And it stopped my sigh.

Wonder if we ever met before?
Somewhere, sometimes together.
The wait is no more;
The trace of you in my heart, I can't ignore.

I searched for hope awhile
When you were gone from me
As hope follows despair,
My memories helped me smile.

But keep me in your heart
To be the reason for your smile
Keep our love alive in your art,
For, someday, we must part.

Your Song

Your song reminds me, Love, of my mother,
A fragile bond I failed to make with the other.

With you, I feel the same connection,
In your song, I feel her affection.

She left me. I wanted to be near her.
Your song stopped me from taking a step further.

Now I don't feel vulnerable,
With you, this loneliness is not miserable.

Every time I play your song, holding a glass of wine,
Away from trouble, life seems beautiful and fine.

From my window, scenery of city lights,
I desire to see this radiant view with you every
    night.

Your song, bringing memories of my mother;
I will keep you in my heart as I keep her.

I miss her, tears come to my eyes.
I feel her whenever I hear *your voice*

Another Chance

Now loneliness torments both of us.
The pain of separation creates a new circumstance.
Don't you think lovers like me deserve another
    chance?

The distance between us is suffocating me.
Please, feel the yearning of my heart,
Come closer to me for a new start.

Don't be ruthless on this stormy night.
Someone here is longing for your second glance,
Give lovers like me another chance.

Empty Street

Walking down an empty street,
A hot wind blows.
Sun shining bright,
I am lost in memory of you.

Roadside café. We used to go
To sip some coffee.
Staring at you there for hours
Was my favorite hobby.

Old books carry scents of the flowers
You bought from here,
The shop near the tower.
Those flowers, for me, a souvenir.

The park where we met
Every evening for a walk.
We witnessed many sunsets,
Talked of our future.

No chance to see you now,

Though I walk here every day.

It keeps *us* near,

This empty street, refreshes memories of you.

A Companion

Unfulfilled dreams are dying on the earth as
    raindrops.
O world, you're a perilous web of hope.
It's too hard to walk alone through the smoke.
Cruel realities extinguish the light of eyes.
I'm not a coward, but I need someone here with
    me to cope,
A companion who will hold my hand in all the
    strife,
A tender heart among these remorseless souls.

Not Alone

You died
And I
Was left alone
In this deserted house.

A few loved ones came and went.
Those who were not able to come
Expressed their grief over the phone.
All were sad for me because I had lost my spouse.

They don't know that you are still with me, that
I am not alone.
You still exist inside me,
You are my strength; you inspire me to live.
Together we will continue to experience
This magnificent ride which we call
Life…

Limitless

Limitless time we fought.
Separated.
We were as different
As I'd thought.

We tried again,
Keeping our egos aside.
Together we smiled and
Cried again.

Millions of reasons
To keep apart. Yet,
Our love binds us
In every season.

Limitless, this life we live.
For you,
Every part of it,
I want to give.

An Illusion

I lived a dissipated life
Until you came along with a magic wand
Or maybe I just followed your command
And all of life's dullness was suddenly gone.

I wholly trusted your decisions.
Your charm cast a spell on me.
It enslaved me, or did I feel freer?
I was completely seized by your illusion.

Your advice settled in my mind
You were endowed with compassion
While caring for me during my abreaction.
I am greatly obliged to you.

Your presence is comforting to me
Your touch is the medicine I was looking for.
In your lap, I can breathe more
Let me stay forever in your fascination galore.

Comfort Zone

Love is a pleasant tickle in the midst of all troubles
Under its shadow, every complicated soul humbles

I haven't learned to live with many a compromise
Life is unrepentant and not as we fantasize

Among these unknown faces, it's you whom I have
known
Your innocent face gives me the feeling of a sweet
home

Living with strangers frightens me sometimes
When you come closer, life brightens every time

Adherence to you can help me cross obstacles
Alone I might not be able to solve life's puzzles

Promise me you will never leave me alone
In this selfish world, you are my only comfort zone.

My Seductive Eyes

Baby, I know

You purposefully stay up late at night

To keep looking into my seductive eyes

My gaze is enough to give you butterflies

It enchants you forever

Baby, you know

I feel our small bed is so wide

But we only take up one side!

A transient distance between us makes you worry,

    right?

You treat me like I'm your sumptuous treasure

Baby, we know

It's not the fault of the room's scattered light

This closeness again keeps us aroused tonight

You are spellbound again by my seductive eyes

As you drown again in their pleasure

A Simple Language

Describe your love in a simple language
Without being naughty
Say it in a way that touches my heart
Don't take a long pause
Being overanalytical dilutes real thoughts.

Don't be too late if love exists
Long waits can change sentiments
Narrate your sentiments like a story
A story in which we are the main characters
To be honest, life is nothing less than a theatre.

Look into my eyes, don't be shy
Your hesitation can destroy my enthusiasm
Express yourself bravely
Let the depiction of your love be romantic poetry
So that I can perfectly know you in your entirety.

Old Bridge

An old bridge where we first met.

Early morning, I come to the same rendezvous.

Haven't seen you in a long time

Perhaps today the misfortune will end, and you
    will come here again

While waiting, I had a flashback.

Remembering the day we saw each other here.

My smile made you feel shy.

The next day, we slowed down our bicycles to say
    "Hi!"

On the third day we stopped at this bridge to shake
    hands

And got to know each other's name.

On the fourth day you bought me a chocolate.

We relished it while looking at the sunflower field.

Remember, those sunflowers were waving like
    flames.

Every day at this old bridge, we started taking a
    short break

Those days were fantastic.

We were enjoying our meeting game.

Then you stopped coming to the bridge.

Left me surprised and concerned.

Every morning, I come here expecting to meet you
again.

My dear, if you're playing with me

Then please return.

I am not liking this new game.

Forever

Among the clouds
The stars twinkle and
I feel grateful whenever you
Come near and whisper
'I Love You'
In my ears.
Our white hair and wrinkles
Are proof of our prolonged togetherness.
We have come a long way
With each passing day,
You are becoming more of mine.
Gone are the days when we repent.
Yes, we are perfect for each other.
Beyond worldliness,
Beyond materialistic things
Beyond greed and selfish needs
Our love keeps growing.
With time it becomes robust.
Every day, you are becoming more of mine

Every day, I'm becoming more like you
Yes, Sweetheart
It's true.

What Have I Done Wrong?

I have lost you

You, my only well-wisher

After you,

I got surrounded by imposters

Never wanted to be acquainted with them.

You were the only genuine contributor

For me

And I lost you.

This peace gives me fear

Sorrow outspread all over

I don't have an appetite

on this forlorn dinner table.

I treated you inappropriately

I'm sorry, my love,

That was not fine.

All the afflictions I gave you

Are coming to me

You walked out

I am suffering alone,

Counting my past crimes.

A Moment In The Downpour

A dim light in the downpour.

The blurred view, my eyes tried to endure

Then you showed up like a rainbow

I tried watching you from the window

It seemed you lost direction

And the rain tested your comprehension

As you walked past my window

In grey weather, you were glowing in yellow

That special moment transmuted the whole thing

You took shelter in my house during the
     turbulence

Now you've become the most valuable ornament

In our home.

Assurance

Lift me up,

I'm dwelling in a gloomy abyss.

Heal me with endearment.

I need your attention every minute.

Proffer a tenderness

Which is rare.

I will transcend all barriers

If you keep holding my hand

And

Never stop showing that you care.

4 pm Meeting

Yesterday you sent me a message
To meet.
I was so happy, I wasn't able
To sleep.
"4 pm at the same restaurant,"
You wrote to me precisely
So, today I finished
All my work timely.
I have reached on time,
And I wait for you.
Drank three cups of coffee,
And there's no sign of you.
Your phone is switched off
How should I feel?
You forgot about our 4 pm meeting,
I am a fool, unnecessarily here,
Waiting…

Success Killed Your Spirit

You became slightly famous
Started getting closer to a life of glamour.
Our fortunes began to change
With a new life you obtained.

Facebook, Twitter, & Instagram.
You were addicted to all platforms
You began flirting with your followers
I expressed my displeasure without showing anger

I tried to take you down the right road.
But you were an egotistic fraud.
You blamed me for no reason and started a fight
You lied to me and chivalrously smiled.

I decided to let you go.
Because I had self-esteem too.
All those dreams that I left for you
I wanted again to pursue.

The two of us are aware of a reality.

That you failed to manage your success entirely.

Hopefully, someday you'll feel guilty.

When you realize that success killed your spirit
    completely.

Last Attempt

Our chaotic love
Those arguments, fights,
Then, make-ups.
You were childish
I was passionate
We were growing collectively
Under each other's care.
Things were perfect
Till we fought for the last time
Then you got desperate to separate
I tried to stop you, but failed
The burden of regrets is the reason
Of my ultimate stress.
I'm sending you an apology mail
I don't care who was wrong or right
I don't want to discuss that old fight
This mail is my last attempt to bring you back
If you ever loved me for real
Come back, I'm yearning for you dear

Novel

You wrote a novel about us.
You made me the villain and
Portrayed yourself
A victim of love.

You deceived readers with your clever words
I chose to stay quiet
Until I saw hate in
The eye of every passerby.

Whenever I go out
They ask questions.
Do I deserve such retribution?
Is it fair to punish me with your work of fiction?

I am so devastated by this.
My love towards you was true and
You're still playing with my heart,
Using me again as a tool of your art.

Midnight Life

A clamorous day, on the way
And always I'm unprepared for it.
An introvert like me, feels disconnected in the crowd
When impassive people speak very loudly.
They aren't willing to hear me.
If I disagree with their viewpoint,
They ignore me with no justification.
This artificial life in the daytime
Doesn't suit my vibe.

A sonorous night, keeping stay a while
For you, I need no formulations.
An introvert like me, always craving solitude.
In silence, I hear my forgotten voice.
I speak to myself for hours.
To grasp my contrasting opinions.
Solitude never distracts me.
Midnight time always attracts me.
It totally suits my vibe.

Silk and Velvet

These charming ladies
In silk and velvet gowns.
Drinking, laughing, enjoying
At the party in town.

I went astray
In the dark.
My wound
Now healing
When these ladies
Come around.

Shimmering eyes, flawless smiles,
And, oh, their nightingale voices.
These angels in silk and velvet,
Lighting up my sky.

I Am a Lone Warrior

I am a lone warrior

A strong soul

Heart made of steel

I will pass all ordeals

I know how to play with zeal

Enemies may be throwing stones, but

I will fight and heal

On the battlefield, I'll follow my deep insight

To survive and to win

World's ferocity can't change my heart

God blessed me with an optimistic mind

Nothing can make me weak

In negativity, I will thrive

Bad times will vanish in the wind.

I will fulfill all my dreams

People who deceived me

For them, I will not cry

My eyes are on the sky

And. I. Have. Wings.

I want to do something great
I know I'm a fighter and I'm brave
People who are laughing today
Will later regret
When they come to my grave

March

March is my month

The month of Spring

Nature shows her full beauty

The birds happily sing.

River water sparkles,

So does my emerald ring.

Warm sunlight touches my skin,

Making me feel like I am wrapped in fleece.

Often I tremble

When a cold wind

Touches my skin.

My mama calls me Spring Baby

Others think I'm a bit crazy

Melancholy, from me, stay afar.

My beaming face

Ample to attract folks.

I was born in March

It's really my month

Vibrant flowers and green mountains

Blue sky, a solace to my eyes.

I feel strengthened

By the unique aroma of each day

I feel recharged when I inhale

This miraculous air.

March never fails

To amaze me.

For me it's nothing

Less than a fairy tale.

The Pub

So much rush

At this over-crowded pub

An evening before Christmas

There are no vacant seats

Many people are standing up

Champagne, whiskey, rum, and treats!

Everyone is having fun

I'm trying to mind my business

But the music is too loud

And I lose my concentration

Behind my seat

A couple argues—they might be breaking up

On another table

An ex-couple sorts their differences and patches up

To the other side of me

Strangers are busy hooking up

A lot happens around

A single person like me
Quietly noticing everything
While I feign working
On my laptop.

Crush

You look hot
While playing basketball
I get goosebumps
Whenever you throw shots.

Your strong arms
Hit hard at the ball
No other player on the field
Can match your form.

You don't know
I never missed your matches
I'm always present in the crowd
To cheer for you.

I like you more than basketball
Hopefully, one day I'll get your autograph.
I will put it in a frame
On my room's wall.

Route Map

Am I going just round and round,
Or am I on the right track?
I am new to this city.
Anyone listening? I need help!

Entangled in narrow roads,
I stopped walking.
Everyone is in a hurry
Or ignoring me because I'm old?

Then I saw a convenient shop.
I started walking.
Now, in an unknown place,
This route map is my only hope

Little Bird

I miss that little bird

She used to come daily

In the morning, mainly

She would keep shouting

Her beak was so sharp

One day she made a few holes

In my canopy

That was tied from the poles.

Little Bird was mischievous

Her actions made me curious

My abandoned canopy

Started letting in sunlight

My attention was pulled to that site

Plants started growing

And flowers were blooming

Unknowingly she taught me

The significance of change

With time, old things

Need to be rearranged.

I started taking care of my place
I also made a bird house
Hung it on the tree
Next to my house
New birds started coming
Whole garden looked stunning
But that little bird never came back
Whenever I sit here
I miss her "quack-quack"

Solo Trip

Trust yourself.
Actualize your capacity
Don't be thwarted.
You will bounce back
From negativity.
People who always question you,
Just ignore them.
Enough! You're so done.
Done! Done! Done!

Take a vacation.
You know the world is beautiful.
Go, explore new places
Taste delicious food
Make new friends.
Spend time with nature.
After all, we are its creatures.
Never forget, we only live once.
Once! Once! Once!

Travelling makes us wise.
It teaches us self-dependence.
You always learn something new
When you go to another country.
Stop thinking, it's time to act
Choose your track
Book your tickets
Pack your bags and just run
Run! Run! Run!

Your family and friends are
Not interested to join
Ok! Don't be sad, it's fine.
Learn to enjoy your own company
Only you can color your own canvas.
Don't cancel your plan.
Go for a solo trip.
Smile! Have some fun!
Fun! Fun! Fun!